C902026710
D0229713

A BEASTLY P VENTURE

MUNCH, CRUNCH, PIRATE LUNCH!

BLOOMSBURY
LONDON OXFORD NEW YORK NEW DELHI SYDNEY

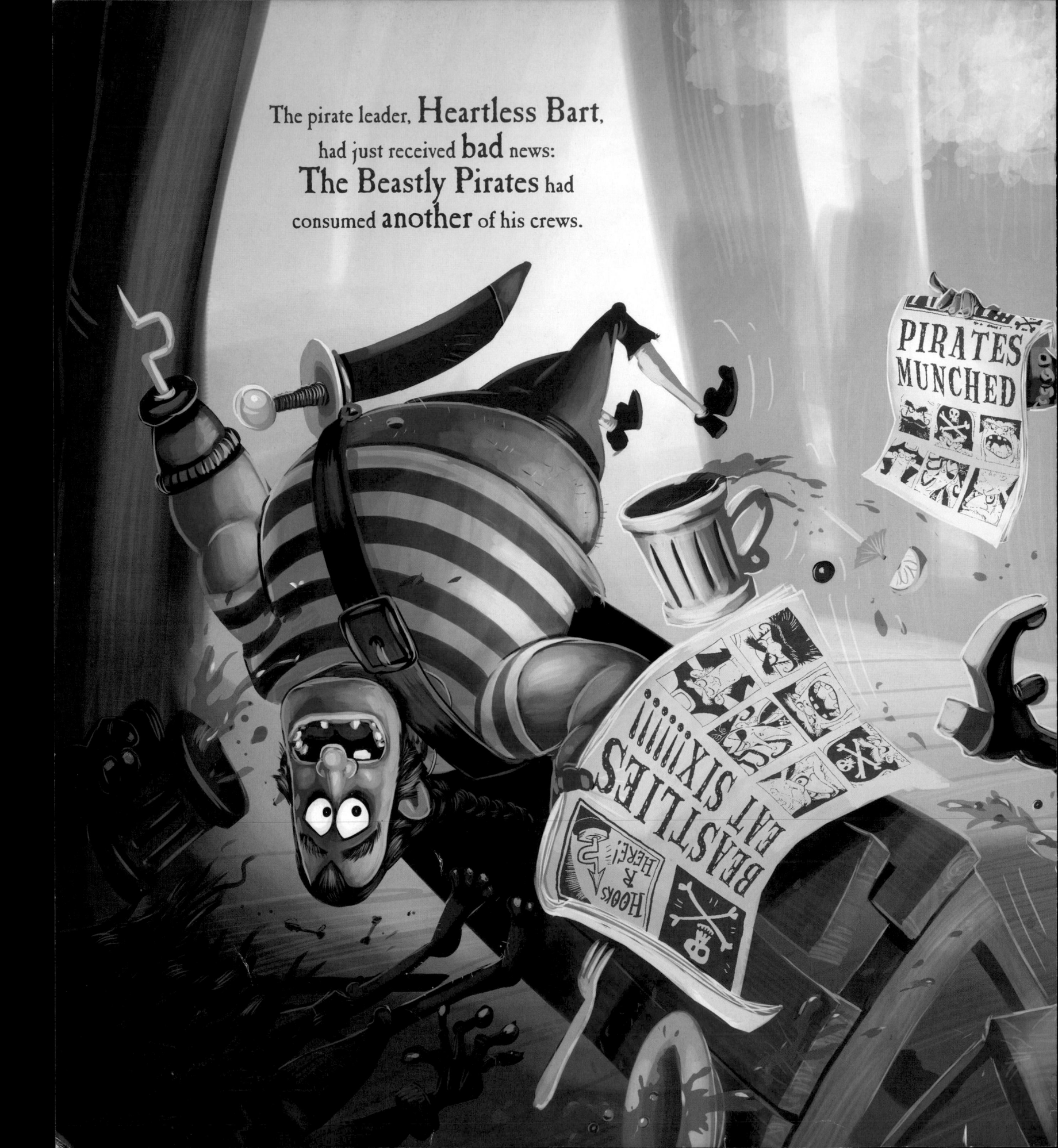

The pirate leader, **Heartless Bart**, had just received **bad** news: **The Beastly Pirates** had consumed **another** of his crews.

"What's wrong with all these
COWARDLY swabs!"
the pirate leader said.
And jammed his giant tankard
tight upon Tom Terror's head.

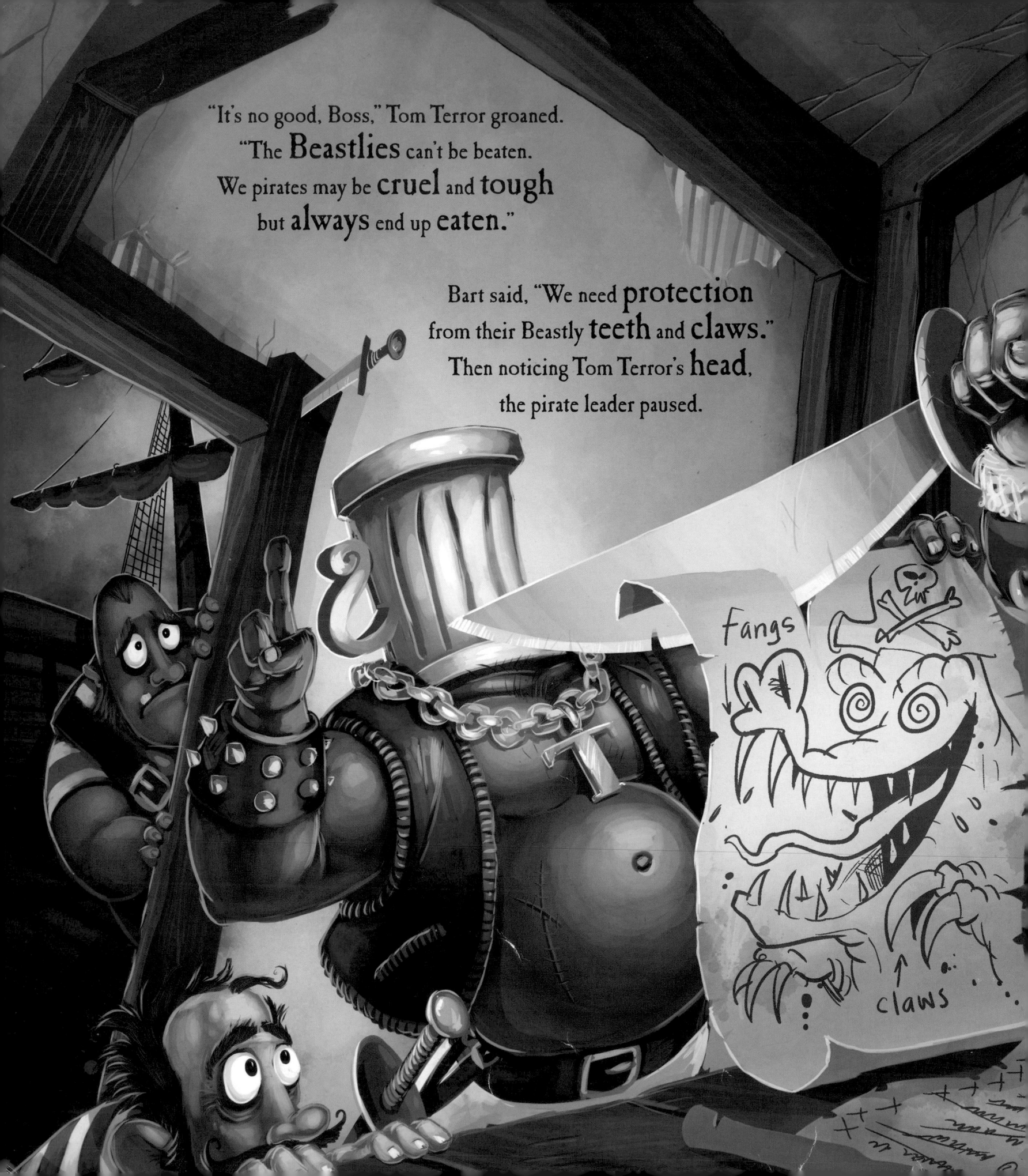

"It's no good, Boss," Tom Terror groaned.
"The **Beastlies** can't be beaten.
We pirates may be **cruel** and **tough**
but **always** end up **eaten.**"

Bart said, "We need **protection**
from their Beastly **teeth** and **claws.**"
Then noticing Tom Terror's **head**,
the pirate leader paused.

"Fetch the blacksmith, right away –
I've had an evil plan!
And round up every sword and axe
and knife and fork and pan."

Five days later, down the coast
and further out to sea,
the good ship Beastly Pirate
prowled the ocean hungrily.

Vic the Vulture squawked,
"A Jolly Roger!
Dead ahead!
It's time for **dinner**, Beastlies.
GET THE OVEN
ON!" he said.

The Beastlies **caught** the pirate ship
but **were** surprised to see
a **giant figure** on the deck,
who **gestured ANGRILY!**

He leapt **aboard** the Beastlies' ship;
there was **no** hesitating.
For Bart was clad
from **head** to **foot**
in **shiny**
armour
plating!

His right hand held a cutlass.
The left a gleaming **hook.**
And painted on his **metal face**
was a **cruel** and **wicked** look.

"I am the pirate leader,"
snarled the muffled voice within.
"Surrender now or
be destroyed.
You know you cannot win!"

"I've come to end the terror
of your culinary reign.
You've had your last pirate repast.
You shan't eat us again."

Razor Rhino
lowered his horn
and rushed Bart
really fast.
But bounced right
off his armour
and embedded
in the mast.
The snarling
Scurvy dog
dived in

and bit Bart
on the bottom.

The metal cracked his
front teeth and he lisped,
"That'th weally
wotten."

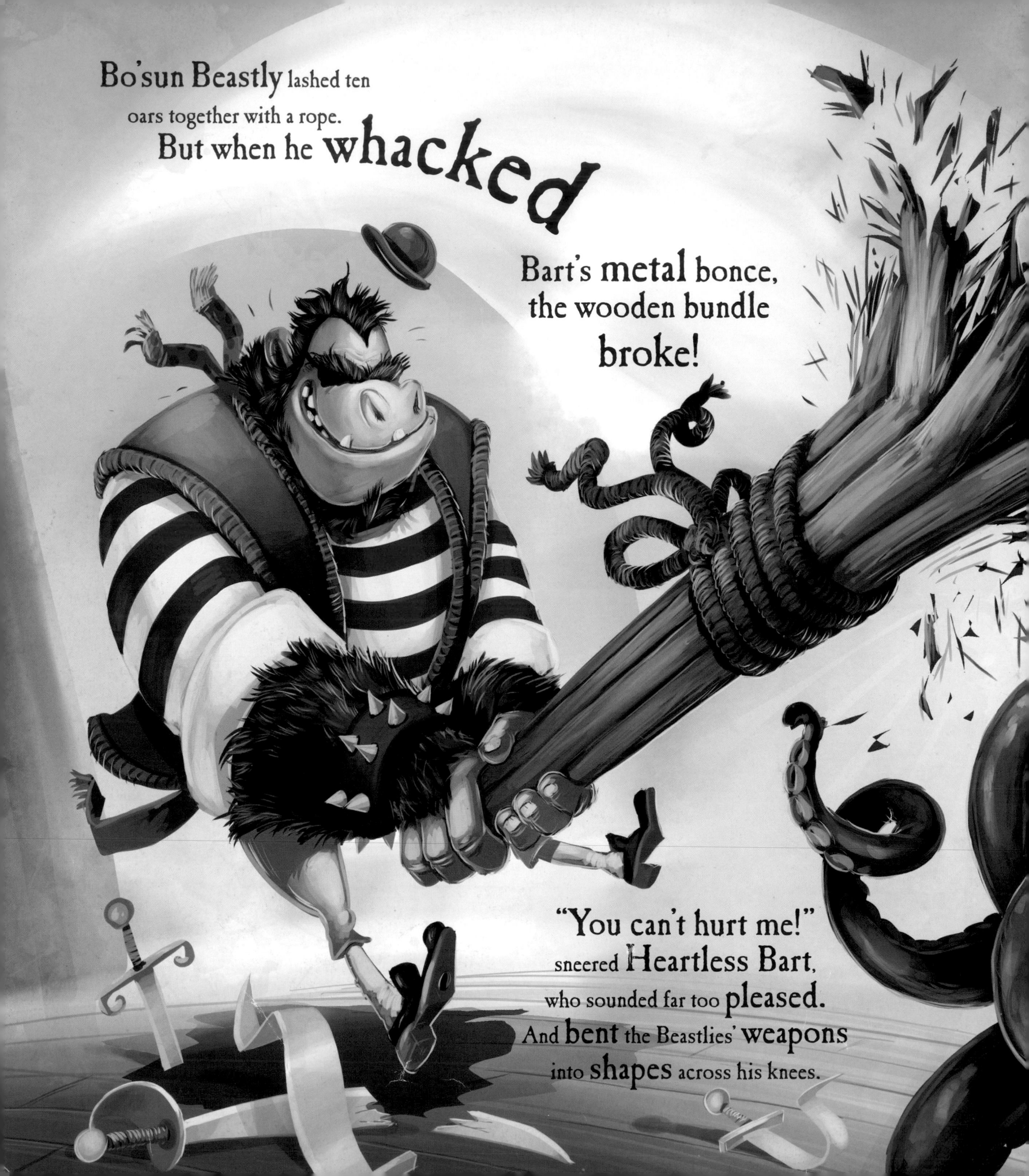

Bo'sun Beastly lashed ten
oars together with a rope.
But when he whacked
Bart's metal bonce,
the wooden bundle
broke!

"You can't hurt me!"
sneered Heartless Bart,
who sounded far too pleased.
And bent the Beastlies' weapons
into shapes across his knees.

Krusher stuck his sticky **suckers**
onto Bart's **cold steel.**
But though he squashed and squeezed
and strained he **couldn't** make
Bart **squeal.**

The Beastlies heaved together
and aimed the ship's main gun.
Then Bo'sun Beastly lit the fuse
and counted...

3...
2...
1...

BOOM!

The cannon ball
bounced
off Bart's **chest**
(but didn't leave a **dent**).

The Beastlies **hacked**
with sword and axe,
but each one **broke**
or **bent.**

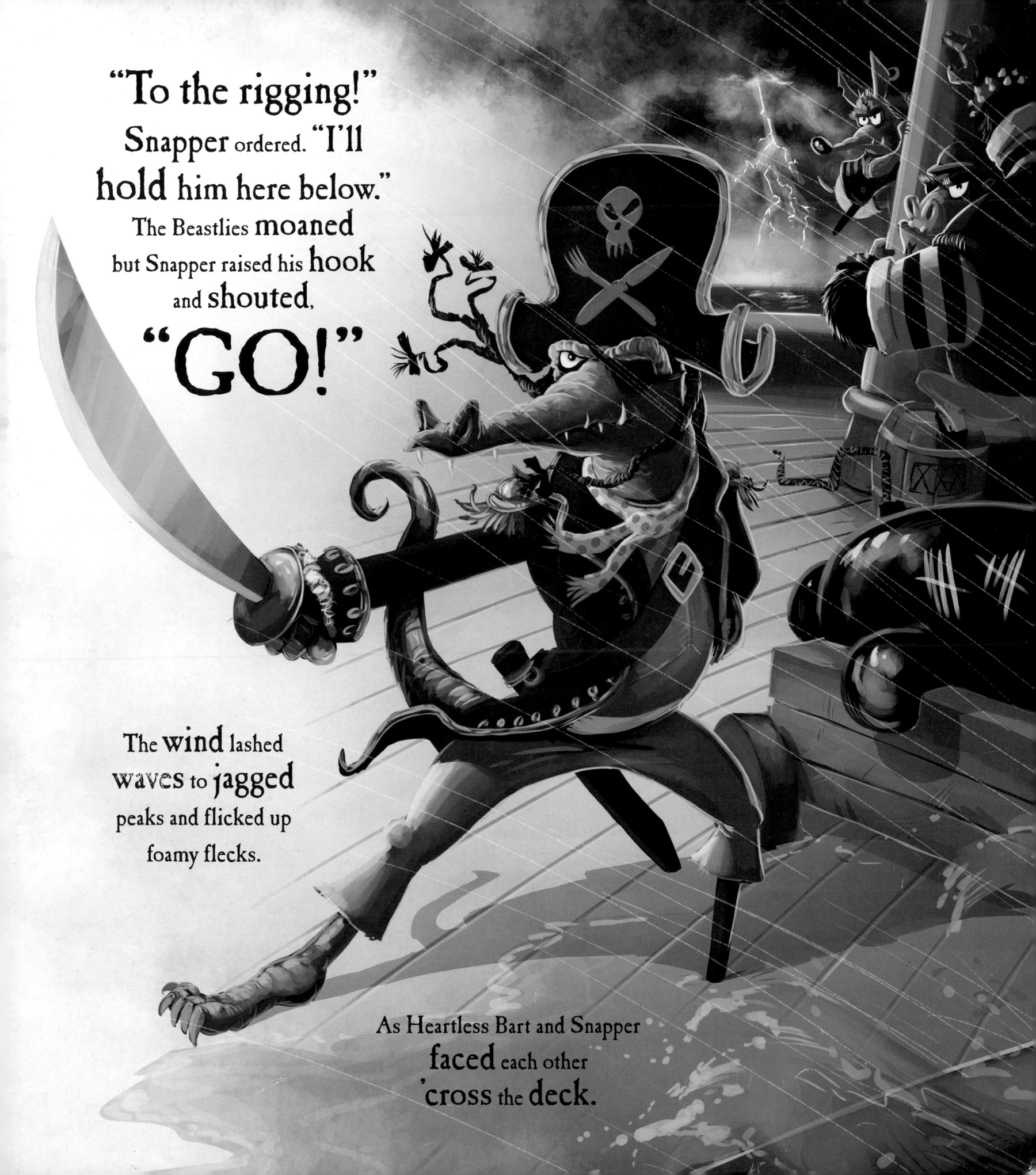

"To the rigging!" Snapper ordered. "I'll hold him here below." The Beastlies moaned but Snapper raised his hook and shouted,

"GO!"

The wind lashed waves to jagged peaks and flicked up foamy flecks.

As Heartless Bart and Snapper faced each other 'cross the deck.

As they climbed
the thunder cracked,
the storm blew from the west.

And every Beastly
squashed and
squeezed into the
ship's crow's nest.

Bart beat him **back**
towards the mast, then with
one **mighty blow,**

he **cut** the Captain's sword
in **two**, and Snapper **gulped**...
"Uh-oh!"

He waited for Bart's **final blow**
but it was **never** dealt.
Instead a **hook** from high **above**
dropped **down** and
snagged his belt.

The cable tightened sharply
and **yanked** the metal bully,
who was astounded when he found
he hung down from a pulley.

The Beastlies dropped **down** to the deck
while Bart shot up the mast!
Up and up Bart went until
the cable **stopped** at last.
He **raged** down at the deck below,
his face **dark** as the sky.

**"Get ready for defeat,
you swabs!"**
and raised his **cutlass** high.
But as he leapt down from the mast
a single **lightning bolt**
struck Bart's sword and
zapped him with . . .

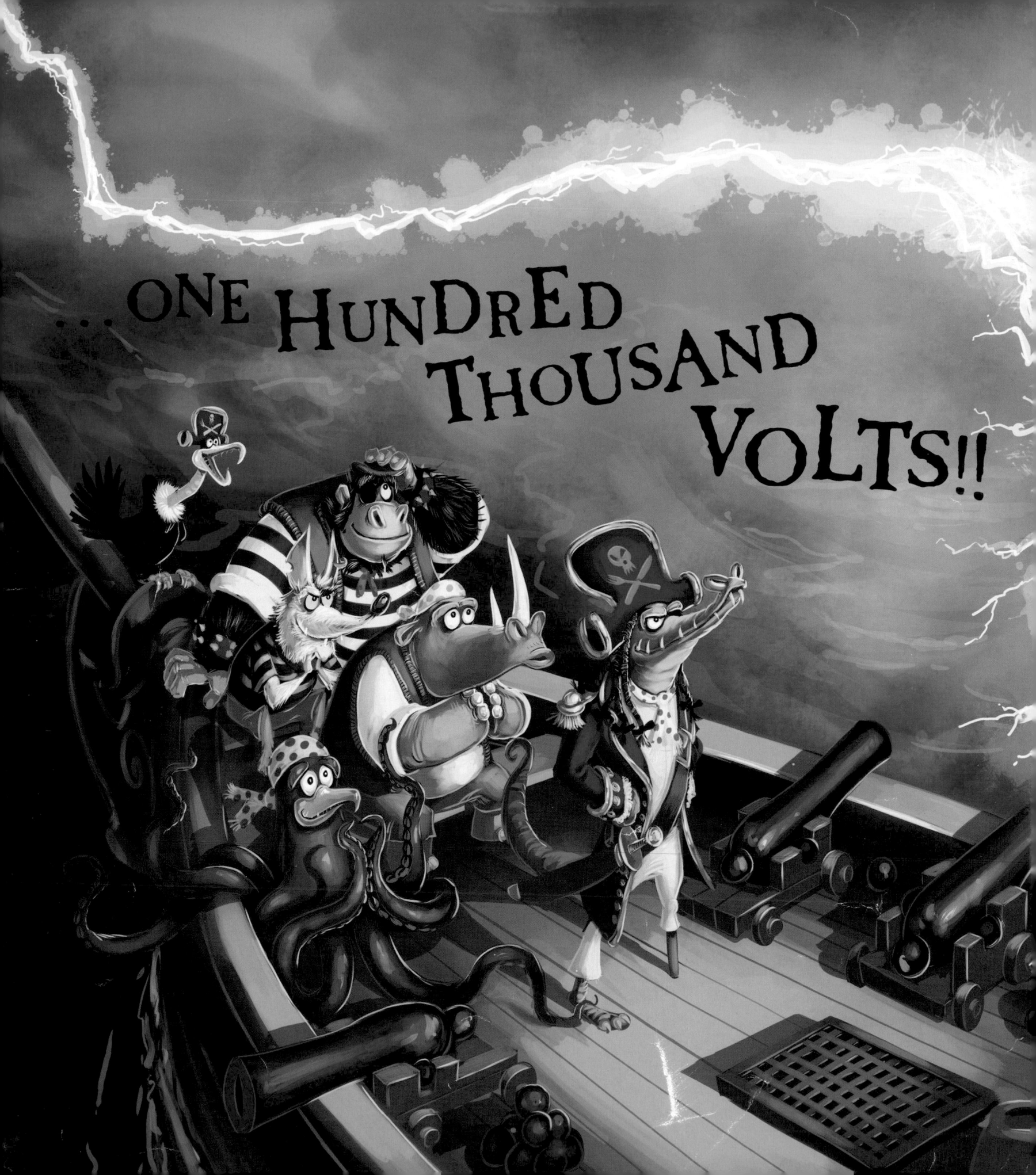
...ONE HUNDRED THOUSAND VOLTS!!

He **tumbled** to the deck **below**
and **landed** with a

CRACK!

Right on his **shiny** metal hat
and **everything** went **black.**

Bart **woke** to find the Beastlies had
cut off his sword and beard,
and **made** the **one** and **only** thing an
armoured pirate **feared.**

A GIANT metal can-opener!

Bart squealed, jumped up and ran.

"HURRAH!"

The Beastlies cheered.

"Our favourite . . .

. . . Pirate-in-a-Can."

One week **later**,
Tom (The Tankard)
still hadn't heard a peep,
since Heartless Bart sailed
away on Wednesday last week.
Tom knew that with his **armour**
Heartless Bart could **never** fail.
And thought the Beastlies
must be dead
when someone yelled,

"You've mail!"

Amongst the **WANTED** posters
and the bills for hooks and rum,
was a **postcard** from the Beastlies
– and it was addressed to Tom!

It said,

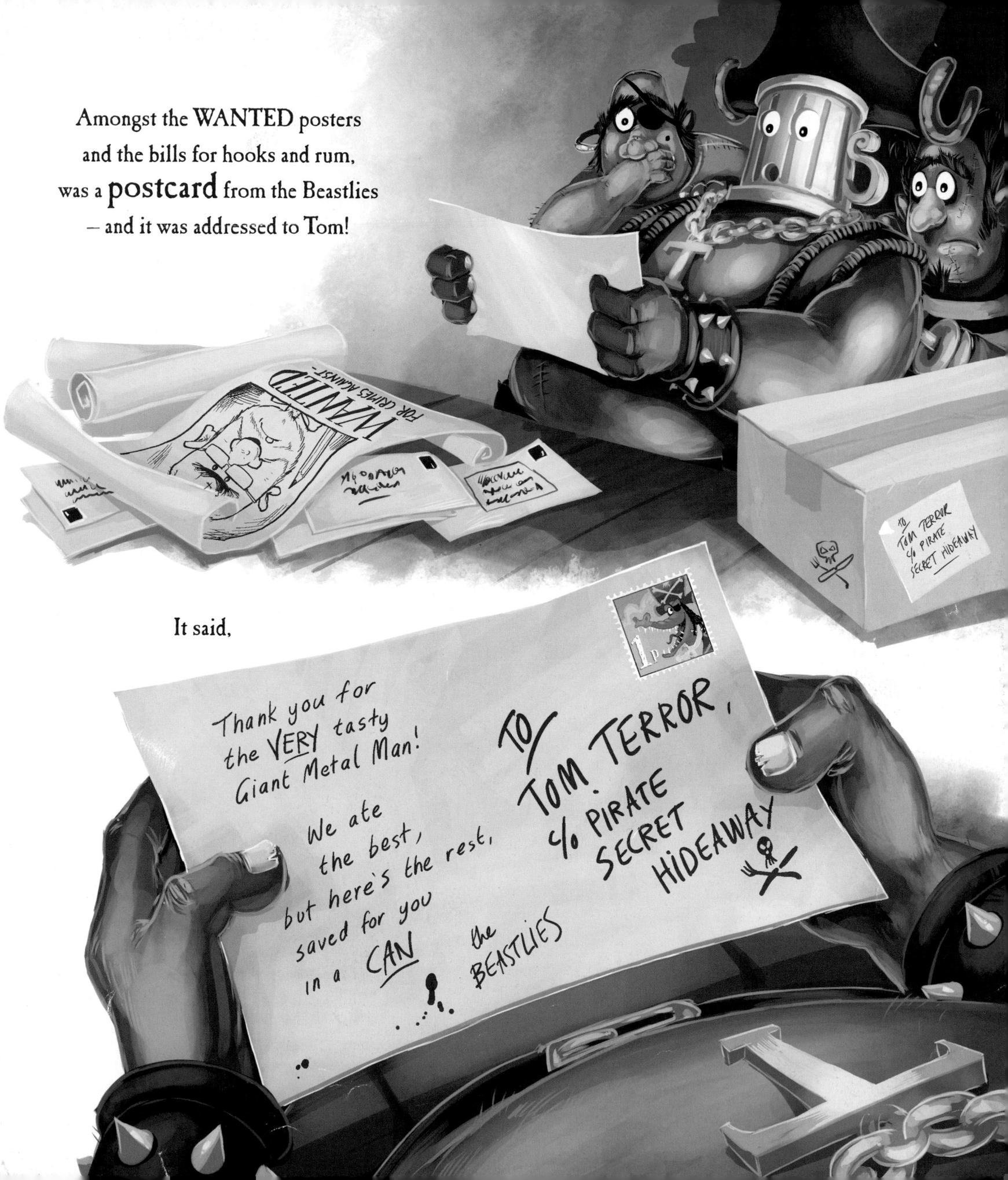

CAPTAIN SNAPPER'S FINEST*
PIRATE-IN-A-CAN
*NO ADDITIVES!